MW00718430

TaleSpins

written by
Michael Mullin

Cover art and illustrations
by John Skewes

ISBN: 978-0-9851884-2-9

Gemiknight
STUDIOS
PASADENA, CA

printed by
Bridgeport National Bindery, Inc.
Agawam, MA

for my Mom
Diane Dawson Mullin
3/5/34 – 7/26/11

who most certainly would have enjoyed these stories

and for Dani, Max and Sophie

my nucleus

TABLE OF CONTENTS

The Previously Untold Story of the Previously Unknown
8th Dwarf

The stories we pass down from parent to child
Were once filled with darkness, but somehow turned mild.
We tweak and revise, and when all else fails
We choose to omit certain crucial details.
Until they're forgotten, and nobody knows
How a story originally, truthfully goes.

Take Snow White, for example. A popular tale
With plenty of unpleasant truths to unveil.
For instance, I'd wager that you didn't know
Seven lived in that cottage

… while one lived below.

It wasn't always that way. They once lived as 8.
'Til he changed into strange: staying up, sleeping late.
He ate less and less, turning skeleton-thin,
And shaved his beard down to a patch on his chin.
He was twisted and moody. A freak to the letter.
Calling him "Creepy" didn't make things much better.

He had nothing in common with his cheerful housemates
Who were always so thrilled about things that he hates.
He had different notions of pleasure and fun
And he never agreed with the way things were done.
But each comment was heard as a selfish complaint
So he kept to himself. He practiced restraint.
But silence just made him a deeper enigma
Confirming his odd personality stigma.

'Til one night at dinner, he'd had quite enough
Of their pointless, dwarfish, merriment stuff.
When a spider crawled slowly across Creepy's bowl,
He grabbed it and showed it and swallowed it whole.
"That does it!" they said, and they locked him downstairs
In a cellar room, cold and in need of repairs.
From there he still heard them, their chatter and feet,
And he saw them through floorboards that didn't quite meet.
He wondered how long they would keep up this game.
After all, he was just living up to his name.

The next morning the seven went back to the grind.
Not one looked back as they left him behind.
"Who needs them?" he asked himself, angry and hurt.
Then he stomped around, kicking his shoes in the dirt.

Night after night, the group showed they were fine
With their choice as they sat down to drink and to dine.
They carried on just as they had done before
And pushed guilt-free meals through a hole in his door.

For weeks it continued with no feelings expressed
Until one afternoon that was not like the rest.
While he sat there in silence beneath the wood floor,
An unwelcome creature came in the front door.
"Hello?" it called out in a voice scared and thin.
A reply was not needed. She just let herself in.
"How rude!" thought Creepy in sheer disbelief,
"Unless she's a criminal. Some kind of thief.
If that is the case then it serves those dopes right
The front door unlatched, yet mine is locked tight!"

He quietly moved to the place in his tomb
Where he got the best view of the ground-level room.
She walked overhead, and he opened his jaw,
Surprised and transfixed by the sight that he saw.
Her bare feet were covered with cuts and scrapes,
But beyond that were far more intriguing shapes.
A layer of wrinkled-up cotton and lace
Covered gentle curves in the negative space.
His mind raced with thoughts not entirely clean
Seeing that which was clearly not meant to be seen.
He thought that perhaps he should look well away
Then answered, "Why should I? They made me this way!"

He tried but he could not get sight of her face
As she moved around, no doubt robbing the place.
She soon moved right toward him, the barefoot brunette
To offer what should be his best glimpse yet.
He readied himself and looked to the sky
But all he got was a c
                      a
                      s
                      c
                      a
                      d
                      e   of dirt in his eye!

Some other sound followed her steps in that room.
A scraping? No . . . sweeping! She was . . . using a broom?
He wouldn't have believed it if he hadn't seen it.
She broke into their home to do nothing but clean it!

When he found he could once again see straight and blink
He heard water and dishes. She was filling the sink.
And when hit by the smell of a slow-cooking meal,
He thought to himself: "Is this lady for real?"
Soon after was silence. There was something amiss.
When the others got home, they'd think he did all this.
They'd think he felt sorry and was making amends.

But he had no such plans
for his seven ex-friends.

Come home they did, and they

and they

At their lame little home with the tidy façade.
He then heard the creak of each wobbly stair
And a girl-shriek confirmed that the Maid was still there!
He heard one of them say: "You can live here with us
If you cook and you clean and you don't make a fuss."

She seemed quite content to accept the raw deal
And made each of them wash and sit down for his meal.

The dinner talk soon turned to party plans.
All she did was show up, and she had seven fans.
They laughed, and he told himself: "Don't get excited."
Because he, for certain, would not be invited.

Did they think he would spook her with one of his faces?
Or touch her in inappropriate places?
He won't even be mentioned, lest the "darling" get scared.
They could have their dumb party for all that he cared.

He was kept up for hours by the night's jubilee.
The dancing and laughing went on until three.

The seven left early for work the next morning
Without mention of him. Not even a warning.
So he watched what he could from down under the floor.
A practice he practiced 'til quarter to four.
That's when a sudden, surprise knock on the door
Came so loud and so firm it was hard to ignore.
He heard a "good day" from some raspy old crow
Then their chat played to him like some radio show.

She was selling a shawl made of cottony lace.
He imagined the interest on the Maid's unseen face.
But she pleaded no money at which thereupon
The old visitor implored her to "just try it on."

The next thing he heard was a gasp and a choke.
The old lady ran laughing, but it seemed like no joke.
When the Maid hit the floor from the senseless attack,

 Creepy's view was turned dark by the shape of her back.

He stood on a stool, thinking: "Oh, what the heck,"
And loosened the shawl's deathly grip on her neck.
He only did it so he might have a story to tell
And to avoid a dead body that would soon start to smell.

The next day around noon the old woman returned.
In disguise, Creepy guessed, for the Maid seemed unconcerned.
She welcomed the stranger again to her home
And took from the villain some decorative comb,
A "thank you" was offered from Queen Unaware
As she stupidly stuck the jeweled thing in her hair.

The Maid (not the sharpest knife in the drawer),
Fell in almost exactly the same spot as before.
Creepy sighed, shook his head, then he got the stool quick.
But only reached the poison comb with the aid of a stick.
When it finally knocked loose, the Maid lifted her head.
She'd no clue that she now had been twice almost dead.

The next afternoon the old woman came back
This time with some sort of fresh-picked, fruitful snack.
Creepy thought to himself: "There's no way she'll partake.
Not three days in a row, for goodness sake!"
The next thing he heard was a THUMP! on the floor.
But today she fell well out of reach, by the door.

As he heard the witch-laugh fade away in the wood,
He struggled with how to do that which he should.
   To escape and see whether or not she was dead
   Or risk getting blamed for her murder instead.

Knowing the seven would be home pretty soon
He picked the old lock with his rusty soup spoon.
He went to the spot wherein face-down she laid
   And slowly turned over the gullible Maid.

All the mysteries of nature seemed to fall into place
As he drank in his first real good look at her face.
Her skin and her hair were like nothing he'd seen.
Her eyes, though closed, were still warm and serene.
His face became flushed. He went light in the head.
   If only this vision of beauty weren't dead.

Her neck like an angel, her chest like a doll
He stared and then – wait! Did it just rise and fall?
"Breathing," he thought. "Could his luck be that good?"
   But her coma was sure to be misunderstood.
   He needed to wake her, but didn't know how.
He called her and shook her and knocked on her brow.
   But still she lay still . . .

                                    which made him think *this*:

That no one would know if he gave her a kiss.

Nothing creepy, just an innocent peck on the cheek
Or maybe the lips. He could practice technique.
His mind raced with pre-guilt and worry and doubt
It was wrong to touch lips with a woman passed out.

He struggled, but did it, just as quick and as kind
As he could, before changing his little dwarf mind.
His heart then erupted with joy and with bliss.
His whole outlook was changed by his one-sided kiss.
It got better. He saw that his kiss had some power.
It was to her eyelids like light to a flower.
They opened. She sat up, returned to full life.
He asked her right then and there: "Please be my wife?"

As she opened her perfect red lips to reply,
He saw a new life in his mind's inner eye.

Together with her all
was happy and good.

They lived in a cottage
in some other wood.

She was set now to speak. His whole body went weak.
But the sound she sent forth was a horrified shriek.

Along with her answer, she made perfectly clear
Her discomfort at even having him near.
The whole thing was unfair. He only came to her aid.
What on earth did he see in this dim-witted Maid?
He told her she'd fainted. Perhaps she was sick.
She needed her strength. "Here's an apple. Bite quick!"

He was halfway back to the cellar door
When he heard the soft thud of her hitting the floor.

All through the night while the seven cried.
He refused to look up from his room down inside.
They never confronted him. Never asked what or why.
They just made arrangements and continued to cry.
He watched them all kneel in their sniffling group-sob.
By the see-through glass coffin (And they call him macabre!)
Wasn't he just as special and different as she?
Just not different in a way that they cared to see.
He vowed that because of their judgmental ways
He would stay in that cellar for the rest of his days.

But resurface he did, just one time more.
In the cover of night, with a tool for his chore.
He approached her and thought, "How pathetic she seems.
No doubt her own vanity painting her dreams."
With confidence and skill, he moved toward her head
Knowing they all thought she was already dead.
With his drill, he bore several small holes in the glass
Spaced evenly and hidden down low by the grass.

"That should do it," he said, pretending not to care.
"She gets everything else. Why deny her her air?"

Some well-to-do guy arrived after that night
He kissed her then claimed her, as if by some right.
It seemed a strange kiss was not "creepy" this time.
If the kisser's attractive, it's not seen as a crime.
Creepy scoffed as he watched them ride happily away.
"Whatever. Who needs her?" was all he would say.

If not for his drill, that guy would have kissed death.
"You're welcome," he commented, under his breath.

The End

The Plight and Plot of Princess Penny

This is the story of Penny Lemieux.
Most of it's strange, but all of it's true.
Or perhaps that should read the opposite way.
We won't ever be certain. (Well . . . at least not today.)

Penny was the Royal Princess of the place
from which she came.
It was one of those oddball, storybook kingdoms
that doesn't have a name.
In fact the only thing she knew was
its location "far away."
"Far away from what?" Penny wondered,
but never bothered to say.

Penny's Dad was King (of course), and that
made Mom the Queen.
As Princess, Penny did her own thing.
Last week she turned fifteen.
Most of the time she kept to herself, and she had
her own personal style:
dark eyeliner, six earrings total and her
crooked, smirking smile.

Her jet-black hair hung over one eye
as it fell around her head.
Her favorite thing was a T-shirt saying:
My Stepmom Wants Me Dead.
She didn't have a stepmom; it was a "fairy tale princess" joke.
She wore it for the stares she got and the shock it did evoke.

Her grade point average was just that: "average."
Her report cards showed mostly Cs.
The kids at school avoided her like she had some
contagious disease.
The collective opinion was that Princess Penny
was just all kinds of mean
And all caught up in what was known as
the "V.I.P. Royalty" scene.
Her reputation was she was vain and
liked things done her way.
They said she tried on shoes and jewelry,
and counted her money all day.

Although indeed Penny had no friends, those other
things were untrue.
People misjudged her left and right from their
ignorant point of view.
When kids talk of one who is not in the group,
it's easiest just to agree.
And repeat the rumors of nasty behavior they
never did actually see.
With confidence (and more than a little frustration),
Princess Penny could surmise
That one girl in particular had started all these lies.

A teenage diva named Darcy DeLupus,
in an act of social survival,
Had targeted Penny as a first-class freak
and called the girl her rival.

The situation annoyed the Princess,
but she didn't let it show.
She simply stayed away from places
Darcy's crowd would go.
You'd think someone with Royal Status
could easily get payback.
But the solution came from an unlikely place:
a convenience store magazine rack.

At the end of a boring article on forest fire prevention,
A quarter-page ad with big bold type caught
Princess Penny's attention.
Reading the headline: "got enemies?" made Penny
feel strangely nervous.
Someone who called herself a witch was selling
an unusual service.

Penny read the ad with haste, just getting the general gist.
Standing in the store, flipping and skimming, there was
some information she missed.
She could see this entrepreneurial witch had
made it her business task
To exact revenge against anyone.
As a client, you need only ask . . .

(. . . and pay the small nominal fee that's due.)
(. . . and sign a contract that placed liability with you.)

Although Penny had no experience with this,
it seemed like a pretty good deal.
Darcy would get what she deserved if this
"dark magic" was for real.
Excited, Penny bought the magazine then rushed home
to answer the ad.
She had a habit of acting on ideas, *then* deciding
the good from the bad.

The next morning she got up before the sun
and filled a modest sack.
Some light provisions for the uncharted walk,
and more for the charted walk back.
Her trek took her into a dark and dreary
(yet stereotypical) wood.
Thick trees and strange noises gave her a chill
she ignored as best as she could.

When she came to a ravine with a rickety bridge,
she stopped to contemplate.
No way could this broken-down, splintered thing
hold even her modest weight.
Before she had time to make a plan, a strange creature
came down from a tree.
A short, wrinkled troll with big bug eyes
and a scraggly gray goatee.
He said his name was Jink, and she saw his teeth
were spotted with moss.
She rolled her eyes and said: "Let me guess. I answer
your question to cross."
Jink looked confused. "I've no mystical questions."
Then he asked the regular kind:
"Why are you here?" "Where are you going?" and
"Whom do you hope to find?"

She didn't care to share her story – or even
her name – with this thing.
Although he probably lived nearby,
what assistance could he bring?
If it weren't for the precarious bridge ahead,
she would have just kept walking.
But she was stuck with the smelly troll
who wouldn't stop his talking.

He insisted that she heed his warnings and
make her intentions clear.
Couldn't she sense the dangerous things
that were dangerously near?
He said she didn't seem the type to have
business in these parts.
She looked more at home at a garden party,
being served fizzy juice and tarts.

"How rude!" thought Penny, who long ago
had learned her right from wrong.
She'd decide for herself (thank you much)
where she did and didn't belong.
These woods lacked a certain pleasantness,
but they were part of all outdoors.
"My business," she finally told the troll,
"is really no business of yours!"

She stepped upon the wobbly bridge,
determined not to show her fear.
Just when she thought he might call out,
Jink seemed to disappear.
On shaky legs she made it across.
The whole walk she held her breath.
Three times a board broke under her foot,
and she almost fell to her death.

She expected a dark and ominous castle
on some treacherous, rocky cliff,
But the witch's address was a quaint little cottage
that made her wonder if
She'd come to the wrong location
or was somehow else mistaken.
Could the resident here cook up evil revenge
that she could have a stake in?
The welcome mat was made of shortbread.
The knocker was a candy cane.

The whole place had a very UN-witchlike quality
that Penny could not explain.
Before she could knock she heard a click,
and the door swung open wide.
A little old lady in an apron dress said:
"Good morning! Please, do come inside!"

Her hostess was not very tall at all.
She and Penny saw eye-to-eye.
Which was distracting for the witch's left one
was milked over with some kind of sty.
The only thing creepier than that it seemed
was her wrinkled, elastic smile.
Penny made small talk about the house and
asked if she'd lived here a while.
She'd been there two years. The previous owner
was part of the local coven,
When two small children came to visit,
there was some mishap with her oven.
That story sounded familiar to Penny,
who was not so easily shocked.
"Poor thing," said the witch, "But I got the place cheap,
and the pantry was fully stocked!"

Penny had to ask an important question,
before things got too bizarre:
"Perhaps … I could see some demonstration
you are what you say you are?"
Offended, the witch's eyes narrowed to slits.
In a harsh-sounding whisper she said:
"Perhaps I could demonstrate thirty-eight ways
that you could wind up dead."
The Princess thought that was a stupid reply.
"Prove it by killing me?
I came all this way to give you a job.
I'm the one paying your fee."

The witch thought for a moment. She had to concede,
the young girl did make sense.
So she turned a stool into a rat instead
(with some razzle-dazzle suspense).
The transformation was impressive, despite the residual slime.
But truth be told, it was the witch's anger
that said this was no waste of time.
In that two-second moment, Penny saw true evil
on the little old woman's face.
A spell was the way to get back at Darcy.
She was certainly in the right place.

Penny explained how she needed revenge on
a girl who was ruining her life.
Spreading lies, pulling pranks and causing all kinds of strife.
The Princess asked: "How much would it cost
to turn her into a rat?"
But the witch just shook her head and said:
"I'd have to advise against that."
She explained how she once made a frog from a prince,
and another she turned into a beast.
As for effective spells, however, she liked
transformation the least.
She mentioned doing it one other time
in the course of recent history.
"Some do-gooder always reverses the spell,"
she sighed with an air of mystery.

Turning her attention back to Penny, the witch
opened the pantry door.
Shelf after shelf of peculiar bottles were shelved
from ceiling to floor.
Perusing the array of magical ingredients,
the witch offered to mix up a brew.
For full-fee, upfront pay, she explained that
one of two potions would do.
The first (a drink) would make this Mean Girl
see the error of her ways.
The other, when inhaled, would produce facial warts
for a hundred and nineteen days.

Penny considered both of the choices.
Was this some morality test?
She took out her platinum VISA card.
"That second one would be best."

The witch nodded and asked for "the element"
as she examined the credit card.
"The who-what-now?" asked Princess Penny,
completely caught off guard.
She discovered she needed a piece of her enemy.
It said so in the ad.
The witch handed the credit card back to the Princess.
No job. No fee. How sad.
"I didn't read the whole thing," Penny confessed.
"Or I read it, and then I forgot."
"Too bad," said the witch. "I need something to work with.
A lock of her hair or some snot."

Penny apologized for not coming prepared
and told the witch she'd return.
Getting some "piece" of Darcy DeLupus
was now her only concern.

On the walk home, Jink showed up again and
followed her most of the way.
And just like before, he wasn't at all
at a loss for things to say.
He scolded her for visiting the cottage.
His patience was wearing thin.
"Don't you read," he pleaded his case, "any stories
like the one you're in?
You pay an old hag to give you lessons
in the fine art of being cruel,
So you can attack some misguided girl
who also attends your school?
Do you think your dark deed will earn you a place
within the popular crowd?
That sounds like a really well-thought-out plan.
Your parents must be proud."

Penny usually appreciated sarcasm, but not from
this eavesdropping elf.
"You don't need a witch!" Jink called as she ran.
"Take care of your problems yourself!"
That's just what Penny thought she was doing.
So what if she got assistance?
Her plan will work just fine if that nosy
troll-thing keeps his distance.

Sooner than expected, Penny got her chance.
After school the very next day,
She found you-know-who with her gang
of friends in a popular café.
There were Brian and Ryan from the soccer team,
and little Annabelle Krupp,
Who followed Darcy's every move like some
well-trained, short-leash pup.
Britney Brady and Peter Fink sat
romantically hand in hand,
And a boy named Trevor was cracking jokes
that no one could understand.

At the center of the group, as if holding court,
were Darcy and her boyfriend Steve.
They held the group's attention in a way
Penny found hard to believe.
Steve was handsome and physically sculpted
like a guy in a billboard ad,
But he was shallow, an insufferable jerk,
whose ego was pathetically sad.
Penny's parents (in the political sense) were
the actual King and Queen.
But Steve and Darcy held those titles
when it came to the teenager scene.

Penny recognized one other kid
from Ancient History class.
They whispered and giggled just loud enough
to make it awkward for her to pass.
The mocking continued as she waited in line
and ordered a jasmine tea.
If it weren't for the necessary task at hand, this was
the last place she wanted to be.

At a corner table she tried to look busy
by taking out some books,
But her peripheral vision told the real story
of the teasing, hurtful looks.
She needed to think of a way to approach without
giving the wrong impression,
In order to make some part of Darcy
become her next possession.
She could ask to borrow a hairbrush and hear:
"Are you from outer space?"
Or shout some taunting insults and hope
that Darcy spits in her face.

While Penny schemed she heard them argue about
homework due the next morning.
None of them had the correct assignment,
so Darcy issued a warning:
"Get me that paper, and get it quick!
This is no longer a friendly chat!"
She yelled at her friends like a witch . . .

(or at least like something
that rhymes with that).

Penny knew the assignment in question
was a long division worksheet.
In a second she found her copy and was
getting up out of her seat.
The whole group stared as Penny approached.
The contempt was hard to ignore.
But Penny just smiled her friendliest smile:
"Is this what you're looking for?"
Darcy glared. Her guard went up.
Why would the Princess help out?
There must be a catch. Some ulterior motive.
Darcy had reason to doubt.

"I guess not," Penny said to the awkward silence,
and then she turned to go,
But Darcy snatched the page from her
to let everybody know
That she was in charge here, and she would decide
when any conversation
began or changed or came to an end.
This was a Darcy Situation.

But the impulsive act made Darcy cry out.
The result was unexpected:
A nasty slice of a paper cut that was
bound to get infected.
Darcy immediately blamed "the Princess"
for causing her finger to bleed.
While her friends (particularly Annabelle)
attended her every need.
Penny took the worksheet back and said:
"I do believe this is mine."
On the page was a quarter-sized stain of blood.
She thought: "That should do just fine."

The next day she journeyed back to the witch
with a sense of expertise.
Even the bridge was magically fixed,
which made crossing it a breeze.
The witch welcomed her with that stretchy smile
and offered her a seat.
If things went well, Penny reminded herself,
they'd never again have to meet.

Seeing the rat from her previous visit
was once again a stool,
Penny imagined how a transformed Darcy
would be an epic kind of cool.
The witch held out her bony hand and
took the bloodstained paper.
She nodded approval then opened the pantry
to prepare the sinister vapor.
This time Penny got a much closer look
at all the bottles inside.
Each one had a clearly written label,
and that was how she spied
On the far left side, about waist high,
a small one with tinted glass,
was labeled: "Transformation".

Could she let this
opportunity pass?

The witch found what she was looking for,
and when she turned her back,
Penny thought "Nope" and slipped the bottle
into her shoulder sack.
She felt a kind of rush from stealing
that made it hard to think.
So she followed the witch, who hummed a tune
all the way to the kitchen sink.

Penny's assumptions about witches were wrong:
first the pleasant house and talk,
Now she saw this witch's "cauldron" was
a stainless steel, stir-fry wok!
The ingredients included insect wings and
a strong-smelling, purple powder.
When heated, the mixture bubbled up thick like
a pot of New England clam chowder.
The witch warned her not to get too close
as she gathered the steam in a vial.

But Penny was still thinking of her stolen bottle,
and a Darcy Frog made her smile.

The instructions were simple: open the lid
where your enemy can breathe it in.
The physical effect will take only seconds,
followed by endless chagrin.
Making a note to look up "chagrin" when she
got back home to the castle,
Penny thanked the witch and apologized again
for her previous visit's hassle.

Her thoughts still occupied by transformation,
Penny was not quite done.
"You said you made a beast and a frog.
What was the other one?"
All the witch said about that spell was that
it would never, ever be broken.
No "love's first kiss" or "seeing the good" or
the touch of some "treasured token."
Clearly the witch did not like having
her handiwork reversed.
Penny concluded she'd better get going
before she got caught and cursed.

Walking back through the woods, Penny finally
felt like she was in control.
She would get her long-overdue revenge,
and she didn't have to sell her soul.
She peeked in her bag at the stolen bottle when
she was far away from the witch.
But at that moment she heard a strange wheezing
rise up from a nearby ditch.
She left the path to investigate and found
Jink bent down on one knee.
"Are you alright?" she called as he stood
and leaned on a nearby tree.
With labored breathing he said he was fine.
Just a mild asthma attack.
"I was up all night repairing that bridge,
'cause I knew that you'd be back."
Penny was a bit surprised and touched
that he'd do a thing so kind.
"Are you still going through with your plan?" he asked.
"Are you that much out of your mind?"

The Princess still couldn't comprehend why
this creature cared so much.
For all she knew, he slept in a cave and ate
leaves and bugs and such.
He told her without being asked:
"A witch's spell is a horrible thing.
You do not want responsibility for the sadness it can bring."
Although she was finally listening to him,
she couldn't bring herself to agree.
"What about my years of hurt and sadness? All the suffering
that Darcy caused me?"
"Determining who deserves what," Jink told her,
"is not within your sight.
Vengeful acts of deliberate cruelty will never set things right."
Pushing her hair from her face, Penny shrugged
and said: "Nice guys finish last."
But she proved his point by making such claims
with no knowledge of his past.

She left him there after making sure his breathing
was back to normal.
She had to hurry, for tonight her school hosted
its annual semi-formal.
When Darcy was crowned "Belle of the Ball,"
Penny would make her move.
She'd use the transformation spell. She didn't care
who might disapprove.

Finding a gown was not a problem; she had
many from which to choose.
She opted for purple, mid-calf length,
above canvas, high-top shoes.
Most girls went with a date or friends,
but Penny would take her chances.
When she got there, her classmates stopped and stared.
(She'd never been to any school dances.)
Darcy and Steve stood, full of themselves,
like a catalog bride and groom.
Penny felt her lunch might make a comeback,
so she stopped in the little girls' room.

The evening dragged on with pathetic songs
about "shaking it all night long."
The awful lyrics and monotonous beats inspired
dance moves that were just plain wrong.
After what seemed like something just short of forever,
Steve and Darcy were called to the stage.
They each got a crown made of golden foil
that made them look half their age.

Reminded of a horror story, Penny imagined
blood dumped on Darcy's head.
But the effects of the stolen, dark-magical potion
would have to be the show instead.
Darcy would soon be a frog . . . or a rat . . .
or maybe some other creature.
She realized she had no way of knowing
the nature of the night's main feature.

Penny made her way through the adoring crowd
with hardly a hint of detection,
When she opened the bottle, a hazy mist
floated up in Darcy's direction.
Onstage, Darcy made a sour face
that proved she breathed it in.
Penny smiled and waited for the awesome
reptilian freak show to begin.

But nothing happened. No transformation.
No slimy long tail or webbed feet.
Darcy still looked like the poster girl
for superiority and conceit.
She locked eyes with Penny, put her hands on her hips
and spoke into the mic:
"Look who's graced us with her royal presence!
It's the Princess we all dislike."

"WHAT DO YOU KNOW ABOUT ME?!"

Penny shouted, but Darcy kept her cool.

"You read letters and numbers backwards and mixed," she said.
"That's why you're dumb in school."

Penny's jaw dropped open in disbelief;
the blood rushed hot to her face.
Darcy had humiliated her again.
She had to get out of that place.
As she ran for the door, she felt the bite
of building, mocking laughter.
It was only a few kids, but Penny had no interest
in seeing what happened after.

Once outside she lost the battle to hold back the rush of tears.
Now the whole school knew the embarrassing truth
she'd kept secret all these years.
She'd been taking tests and doing therapy to help
what was wrong with her brain.
"Not wrong, but *different*," her parents would say
to comfort and explain.
But words like that never helped her much.
There was no comfort to be found.
She took out the potion (the one she paid for)
and smashed it on the ground.

How could that spell leave Darcy unchanged?
What the heck was going on?
Unless that "witch" was a scam-artist thief,
running some kind of con.
The rat-from-a-stool was smoke and mirrors!
A parlor trick! She knew it!
But the sad truth was, there was no going back.
She had her chance, and she blew it.
On the way home she vowed to quit school
and stop speaking to everyone,
She had no idea that her night of surprises
had only just begun.

At the castle gate was Jink the Troll,
looking worried and distinctly unclean.
Knowing he was an eavesdropping stalker,
she figured he saw the whole scene.
Penny didn't want his "I told you so" lecture,
but that speech was not on his docket.
He produced a tissue that was surprisingly fresh
(given the general filth of his pocket).

"Thanks," said Penny as she wiped her eyes,
not wanting him to see her so sad.
He did fix that bridge, and now he's here with a tissue.
Perhaps Jink wasn't so bad.
When he said: "I suspect some important parts
of your story remain untold."
She conceded: "You have that talked-about wisdom
that comes with being old."
He flapped his arms in a tantrum of sorts,
as if controlled by a stealth puppeteer.
"And you have the judgmental ways of a teen!
I'm much younger than I appear!"

Penny shrugged her bony shoulders.
Like she cared when Jink was born.
But he had been nice, so she told him this
and tried not to make it forlorn.
"When we were kids, Darcy and I were
inseparable best friends.
Then we had a falling out
with no effort to make amends."
She looked at Jink as if to say:
"That's it," but he held her stare.
"Wow! What vivid detail!" he exclaimed.
"I feel like I was there!
One minor suggestion – just thinking out loud.
I hope it's not absurd,
But you might want to try expanding the part
where *something actually occurred*."

She hated the way Jink called her out
and made her think things through.
With nothing to lose, she told the whole story
(which happened to be true):

I told Darcy about my learning problem.
How it bugged me like a curse.
Reading letters and numbers was sometimes hard,
and other times it was worse.
She vowed to keep my secret forever.
She even helped in each early grade.
Then one day she told me the time had come
for my side of the trade.
I realized her help – and even her friendship –
were half of some twisted deal.
She had a design for a "social system"
she was anxious to reveal.
Created so classmates would know their place.
She saw status as a thing to enforce.
When I asked her where our "place" would be,
she said: "Duh! On top, of course!"
I told her I'd never be part of such a
conceited, mean-spirited plan.
And from that moment on, everything changed.
Our enmity began.

When Penny finished this second version,
Jink seemed satisfied.
But she still couldn't figure out why he cared,
no matter how hard she tried.
He said he was sorry that happened to her.
When she brushed him off, he asked:
"Why do you think you're the only one
with a troubled, unfortunate past?"

"It's not that," she assured him as she opened the gate.
"I've just got a lot on my mind.
I appreciate you coming to help me out.
You've been a pest, but not unkind."
She was still upset that the witch was a fraud,
and she'd gotten a very raw deal.
But Jink said he knew from personal experience
the witch's magic was real.

All wrapped up in her own life's disaster,
Penny didn't get the hint.
She couldn't help thinking he needed a bath
(or at least a strong breath mint).

Jink didn't know what else he could do.
Should he drop to his knees and plea?
"Then maybe there's something," he finally muttered,
"that you could do for me."
Penny couldn't believe her ears. "So you were nice
to get something in return?
Gee, where have I heard that before?"
she added with a glare of spurn.
"No, no," Jink insisted. "You misunderstood.
I'm not that kind of guy."
But the turn of her back and the slam of the gate
said clearly: "goodnight and goodbye."

Inside the castle, Penny snuck upstairs so her parents
wouldn't know she was there.
Which was a bad idea, for in her room she found
the witch in her reading chair!

She'd abandoned the "grandma's kitchen" look
and was now dressed all in black.
When she asked: "How's my little thief tonight?"
she gave Penny a panic attack.
Before the Princess knew what was up,
the room filled with crimson smoke.
When it cleared she was back in the witch's cottage
and realized this was no joke.

She found herself locked in an iron cage
that hung from a ceiling beam.
So frightened was Penny by the turn of events,
she'd forgotten how to scream.
Not that a scream would have done much good,
out there in the darkened forest.
It was not like she'd be found and saved
by some conveniently passing tourist.

The witch held the bottle Penny stole from her
in her spotted, wrinkled fist.
She laughed. The bottle was obviously mislabeled.
This was a truth-telling mist!
The ancient, all-natural spell gets an honest answer
to any one question.
"But that's neither here nor there," the witch added.
"Tonight's about your indiscretion."

But Penny didn't remember asking a question
when Darcy was up on that stage.
Then it came to her: *What do you know about me?!*
she'd yelled in a fit of rage.
The potion kicked in, the secret came out,
and Penny was crushed with shame.
And the worst part was, Penny made her own mess.
She had only herself to blame!

In the kitchen the witch set out four small bottles,
the wok and a mason jar.
She looked like an eerie, late-night version
of a Food Network TV star.
She returned to the pantry and rifled through bottles,
knocking her hat askew.
"I'm out of snakeskin," she called to Penny.
"Did you happen to steal that, too?"
Penny called back an emphatic "no,"
like a well trained eagle scout.
The witch walked to the cage and stroked Penny's hair,
then rudely plucked one out.
"You won't be needing this," she said in a voice
that was way too lighthearted.
"Sit tight," she added, "I'll be back before morning.
Then we'll get this party started."

The witch hobbled slowly out the cottage door
with a laugh that made Penny feel ill.
A minute later she heard a BUMP at the window.
A small, grubby hand grabbed the sill.
Penny knew it was Jink even before he climbed up
and fell clumsily into the room.
She hoped for a rescue, but after their last meeting
she knew she couldn't assume.

He repeated his speech on the dangers of witches
with all of their spells and potions.
"You can't be in charge of ruining a life," he said.
"No matter how strong your emotions."
"Perhaps we can talk outside?" she pleaded.
Each second her hopes were diminished.
"If I don't get out of this cage very soon,
my days as a human are finished."

"Wouldn't that suck," muttered Jink to himself
as he took down the key from its hook.
When he told her she had to stay locked up, Penny said:
"Thanks, but I'd just rather book."
"To where?" he asked her. "Back home to the castle?
Do you really think that's wise?
A person who crosses a witch more than once
is a person who usually dies."
In Penny's opinion, any plan beat waiting
for the crazy witch to return.
"You weren't safe the last time you were home,"
he reminded. "Are you ever going to learn?"

Penny found it odd that Jink knew so much.
He went straight to the hidden key.
Then her eyes went wide with the spark of discovery.
Could it actually, possibly be?
Jink's story was sketchy. He wasn't exactly
good at communication,
So she asked: "Are you what she wouldn't talk about?
Her other transformation?"
He offered a sad kind of smile and nodded
enough to remove any doubt.
"Maybe," he said, "you can help me,
now that you (finally) figured it out."

Jink explained how he couldn't talk about
the things that had happened to him.
It was a condition of the spell cast years ago,
which made his life grim (and Grimm).
Excited, Penny said: "We just need a 'do-gooder'
to reverse the spell and you're free."
Jink sighed with exhaustion making Penny realize:
"Oh, wait. The do-gooder. That's me?"

Jink touched his nose and pointed to her,
then gave her an all-knowing wink.
It was time to inspire Princess Penny to action
(before she had time to think).
He stood on a chair and spoke in earnest,
like a king in a Shakespeare play:
"The witch is the enemy. She must be defeated
before the break of day!"
"Defeated?" asked Penny. "Are we playing checkers?
That kind of plan seems futile."
"That's fairy tale speak for killing," he told her.
"The method can even be brutal."

"How do we do that?" Penny asked.
"With her magic and me in here."
She found it doubtful that a worthwhile solution
would suddenly appear.
Jink told her she wasn't alone in knowing
the witch had magic for sale.
"I ordered a Rigor Mortis spell and
sent the element by mail.
I secretly watched her make the brew
so the process was crystal clear."
Penny listened, but couldn't help thinking to herself:
"What mailman comes out here??"

"When she was finished," Jink continued,
"I made the spell on my own,
Using an element and stuff I took from the witch
and a cauldron I got on loan."
"So you stole from her, too?" Penny asked in surprise.
"Then how come I got caught?"
"I didn't take whole bottles," Jink replied.
"My actions came after some thought."
"Whatever," said Penny. "Can't we splash her with water?
If she melts, that would be ideal."
Jink took a small bottle from a fold in his sock, and said:
"Focus. And please . . . get real."
He popped off the cork and added small pieces
of what looked like dried-up fruit.
Penny's mind wandered. "So before the spell . . .
were you, like . . . you know . . . cute?"
"I'm not a prince, if that's what you're getting at.
The spell wasn't meant for me."
Jink rolled his eyes at the silly question.
"Never mind," she said sheepishly.

"So if we 'defeat' her," Penny changed the subject,
"your spell will be reversed?"
"That's what I'm hoping," Jink shrugged in reply.
"But first things must come first.
When the witch comes back, I must calmly and cooly
pour this on her head."
"Calmly and cooly?" Penny skeptically asked.
Then thought: "That's it. I'm dead."
He explained as the potion soaks into her skin,
the witch won't be able to move.
"And I stay locked up?" Penny asked in a tone
that showed she did not approve.
Jink nodded. "I can't let you out. Don't you see?
She can't know that anything's changed."

said the witch as she stood in the door,
holding snakeskin and looking deranged.

Penny screamed like a banshee, then Jink did too,
and he let the bottle fly.
When it smashed on the witch's big black boots,
Penny felt herself starting to cry.

The witch, on the other hand, laughed then yelled:
"You're done, you little brat!"
"And as for your plan," she sneered at Jink.
"My spells don't work like that!"
With evil in her eyes (Penny knew that look!)
the witch turned for the pantry door.
But she only bent in an awkward twist.
Her feet were stuck to the floor!
She writhed and cursed, but they wouldn't budge.
The potion had taken effect!
When her legs froze, Jink yelled: "It's creeping up!"
And they all knew that he was correct.

"You *fools*!" the witch shouted. She tried to sound mean,
but she was clearly in a panic.
When the spell reached her waist she flailed her arms
in a way that was wildly manic.
Jink and Penny watched in awe as the
rigor mortis continued to rise.
The all-powerful witch was being "defeated"
right before their eyes.
Suddenly Penny had a panic of her own,
and she rattled the iron lock.
"The key!!! Let me out!!" she shouted at Jink
who stood frozen aghast in shock.
He snapped out of his trance and set Penny free
as the spell froze the witch's left arm.
Penny raced to the pantry and grabbed a potion
before the witch bought the farm.
She held the open bottle to the face of the witch,
who turned her nose at the stink.
Knowing the vapor had entered her lungs, Penny yelled:

"HOW DO YOU REVERSE THE SPELL ON JINK?!"

The witch's eyes widened in angry surprise.
She'd been duped by her own truth mist!
Through gritted teeth she answered the question,
despite her attempts to resist:
First you must wait for a crescent moon,
and while wearing a true king's crown.
(Jink thought the instructions might not be simple,
so he scampered to write them down.)
You must hold eight apple seeds under your tongue
and submerge yourself in a lake.
You only have one chance to get it right.
The spell's permanent if you make a mistake.

With that, the stiffness rose up her neck
and past the point of her chin.
She fell silent (of course) then her eyes iced over
as the blood drained away from her skin.
Penny and Jink just stood and stared,
not believing what they had just seen.
The witch now looked like some spooky decoration
you'd put out on Halloween.

"Thanks," Penny said and she patted Jink's shoulder.
"You pretty much saved my life."
"I'd say we're even," said Jink, showing his notes.
Then he took out a pocketknife.
He cut pieces of rope and wrapped up the witch
leaving just a little slack.
Penny saw he was making some kind of harness
to carry the corpse on his back.
"You should get home," Jink said to the Princess.
"Your parents will be worried sick.
I'll bury the stiff somewhere deep in the woods.
I brought my shovel and pick."

Her fear was gone, but a new kind of nervous
made Penny want to joke.
She knew Jink had a sarcastic side,
so she couldn't resist one poke:
"When you threw that bottle, was that 'cool' or 'calm'?
It was hard to know for sure."
"Shut it," said Jink. "Your scream freaked me out.
It wasn't exactly mature."
"Point taken," said Penny. The pace of her heartbeat
had just then begun to slow down.
"We'll meet Tuesday night at Whisper Lake.
You bring the seeds, and I'll bring the crown."

The next night Penny hung out by herself,
which was pretty much routine.
(A decaf tea and a YA novel about
a vampire who was half machine.)
Tuesday was only two days away,
but to Penny it seemed like longer.
She'd noticed her feelings for Jink as a friend
went from zero to something stronger.
She thought about taking a walk in the woods
and perhaps running into him there.
But that seemed lame. She didn't *like-like* him.
And he probably didn't care.
On Tuesday night she'd help him change back
to whatever he was before.
Then they'd part ways, and she'd have to
deal with an all-out Darcy war.

Her return to school the next day, however,
was not what she expected.
Instead of an insult, Darcy said "Hey."
(which Penny figured was misdirected.)
"I don't know why I told your secret,"
she continued with a look of guilt.
She seemed to be truly, believably sorry –
yet that wasn't how Darcy was built.
"It actually wasn't your fault," Penny told her.
"I'd explain, but it's complicated."
Then out of nowhere came that jock-strap jerk.
The one whom Darcy dated.
"You buggin' my girl?" Steve barked at Penny,
who rolled her eyes at the threat.
"It's fine," Darcy growled, then she shooed him away
before she got too upset.
"She's still stuck-up," Steve said as he left.
"I thought that was well understood."
Penny thought a mirror and a dictionary
might do him a world of good.
"Anyway," Darcy tried to continue,
but struggled for words to say.
When she managed a "well" and a "yeah,"
Penny grabbed her books and replied: "Okay."

As she walked to class, Penny tried to imagine
what looked like it could be a truce.
But was she just supposed to forgive and forget
all the years of bullying abuse?
She hoped it was sincere, but had to take
everything into consideration.
Like the idea that perhaps this new Friendly Darcy
was just an affectation.

That night, when the moon showed its crescent form,
Penny made her way to the lake.
(Penny's father, the King, thought crowns
were "flashy," so his was easy to take.)
She found Jink on a rock on the eastern shore,
fidgeting like a nervous wreck.
Instead of "hello," he called over to her:
"Where were you? You're late. What the heck?"

"I am?" thought Penny, knowing the moon
and the lake weren't going anywhere.
But she didn't come to tease or argue;
that wouldn't exactly be fair.
Worry and fear put a look on his face
that was oddly cold. Even ruthless.
He respectfully took the crown from Penny and said:
"Thanks." Then added: "Let's do this."
Walking in so the water was up to his knees,
he suddenly stopped as if stuck.
Penny waded in too and stood by his side.
Then she kissed his cheek for luck.
He took out a pouch that had the eight seeds,
plus several more reserves.
In case he dropped and lost any of them
(which of course, he did, due to nerves).
As the correctly counted number of seeds
were carefully fixed in place,
Penny felt sad this might be the last time
she'd see his ugly face.

When he dunked himself under, the water
glowed green like a radioactive slime.
Something magical was definitely happening,
and Penny wondered how much time
did he need to hold his breath before the
"re-transformation" was done.
Whatever happened, she knew the witch was dead,
and that she and Jink had won.

After what seemed like the longest half-minute
Princess Penny had ever endured,
Jink stood up, all wet and panting, and Penny thought
he looked (*ahem!*) . . . cured.
His dark, curly hair spilled from under the crown.
He had blue-as-a-summer-sky eyes.
He was so unlike the Jink Penny knew,
the change caught her a bit by surprise.
Besides the obvious, physical attraction,
there was a hint of recognition.
There was something familiar in his
bookishly charming, rock star-restored condition.

When he took off the crown and handed it back,
it came to her sure enough.
He looked like Darcy's boyfriend Steve,
only not as coiffed and buff.
She must have said "Steve" out loud without knowing
as they stood and stared at each other,
Because Jink nodded and responded by telling her:
"Steve is my older brother."

"Steve is your what-now?" Penny asked in a way
that put a strange look on her face.
Jink smiled. "The witch didn't like how he acted,
but I volunteered to take his place."
It made sense to Penny, because Steve was a jerk
like those others the witch had cursed.
"I tried to negotiate," Jink said with a shrug,
"but she refused to be coerced."

The way these stories go, Penny recalled,
they should now be in love and kiss.
She fearfully wondered if Jink thought that too,
so she offered a quick: "How about this? . . .
You come to school (after a good long shower
and a change into normal clothes).
We'll hang out, walk to class, sit together at lunch.
We'll just see how it goes."
Jink was fine with that slow-speed plan.
He'd been out of the loop for a while.
He was scared to death to be part of a couple,
but he agreed with a confident smile.

And that's how it went the next day at school.
Jink and Penny shared quality time.
What a pleasant change to have neither tormentors
nor social ladders to climb!
At their lockers Darcy accosted Penny
and asked her: "Who's your friend?"

"Don't even," said Penny as her story
came to what is for you, the reader,

The End

It's become quite a trend to take a known story
and tell it a different way.
That's all well and good, for we can assume
every author has something to say.

A changed point of view or a whole new character,
created to "set things right."
I know nothing of that, but the story that follows
did happen to me one night.

If you must know I'll tell you that I am a doctor.
Little else will be revealed.
I'm too modest to say, but others
have called me a giant in my field.

A certain luxurious way of life
has been gained from my success.

The entire top floor of a high-rise
serves as my permanent mailing address.

Over the years I've collected some treasures
from travels all over the earth.

Paintings and artifacts added to the fortune
I received as a right of my birth.

I'm not one to brag, so please understand,
my wealth is a relevant fact.

For someone broke into my home that night,
and I got (as kids say today) "jacked."

PART I

I'd spent several hours at work that night
inside of someone's head.

Quite literally. In surgery. When they brought
him to me he was minutes away from dead.

But I did my job with experienced skill
and repaired the poor guy's brain.

I left the room, my hands and back
in a twist of arthritic pain.

The next half hour was a windshield blur,
a trail of street lamps home,

where the ritual of my arrival includes
some time with a garden gnome.

That's just what I call the short and pudgy,
white-bearded operator,

who spends his days pushing numbered buttons
in my building's elevator.

But that night the odd-looking senior citizen
was not in his corner space.

A punkish teen wore the tassled uniform
and did the job in his place.

On his coat I saw the brass oval tag
that told me his name was Jack.

When I asked about the gnome, he just said: "Died."
Then: ". . . heart attack."

He mumbled something else that I ignored.
I was having a moment of mourning.

Inside my apartment, I walked right past
what should have been a warning.

It wasn't until I was set for bed
that I noticed something wrong.

Several of my treasured artifacts
were not where they belonged.

I wondered who would bother to invade my home
to rearrange my art collection.

Then I saw one glass case was broken and empty.
The thief had made a selection.

Shards of glass led a Hansel and Gretel
trail all the way back to the door.

(These light-catching pieces were the obvious "warning"
I should have noticed before.)

The stolen item was an emerald sculpt
of a stalk growing out of the earth.

"It represents the soul," the artist had told me,
adding mystery to its worth.

I called the police, and a tired officer
took my detailed report.

Step two was to reprimand "building security"
for efforts which clearly fell short.

The elevator came, and (big surprise)
the teenager was not at his post.

I pictured him shirking, in a text conversation
that had him completely engrossed.

With annoyance, I pushed the button myself
and grumbled through my descent.

A chill hit my body for one brief moment.
I had no idea what it meant.

Countless times that elevator had taken me
down to the ground.

But this ride was different. I can't say how,
but when I took a look around,

the world had changed (or at least the lobby)
as far as I could tell.

A dreamlike haze washed over the scene
as if conjured from some sort of spell.

I overheard the manager apologizing.
He and his staff were remiss.

He vowed with a fatherly shake of his finger
to "get to the bottom of this."

His mention of staff made me think of
the newest, the kid I had already faced.

What if the gnome had indeed passed away,
but had not yet been replaced?

"That was easy," I thought to myself,
convinced I now knew the thief.

The officers who arrived ignored my theory.
I was stunned with disbelief.

The bustling chaos of police (and an ambulance?)
was a peculiar thing to see.

In fact, it seemed everyone at the scene
had some interest other than me.

I heard someone sneeze as I walked outside.
Perhaps I'd spot the guilty young man.

From the alley I heard the distinctive rattle
of an aerosol spray paint can.

I followed the sound and saw a graffitist
defacing a nearby wall.

At first the can looked oversized,
then I realized he was strikingly small.

"Who are you?" I called as I approached,
But he didn't look up from his work.

I knew he heard me; the sound of my voice
stretched his mouth in a wise-guy smirk.

He'd written

and tagged it "FeeFye"
in a swirling silvery white.

As I read it, he was painting another message
a little further down to his right.

"What is this?" I asked, but he just laughed.
Like a rodent he scurried away.

I couldn't chase him, so I stopped
and took in his entire artistic display.

The alley filled with a thick, cold mist.
My face and my fingers went numb.

In red, shadowed letters, his other message read:

and was tagged "FoFum".

A door then appeared underneath each message.
They were painted, yet somehow real.

It looked like a carnival side show attraction.
"Step right up" (if you knew the deal).

Two similar sentiments with different tones.
They were asking which I wanted to do.

I was surprised to see the door beneath my choice *open*.
I took a deep breath and walked through.

PART II

Getting into the penthouse was easy enough.
But I had no idea he had so much stuff.

A huge collection all on display.
Most were too big to haul away.

Near a naked-guy painting I found offensive
was an interesting sculpture that looked expensive.

Green-jeweled leaves on a little sprout.
Now that was something I could carry out.

It'll turn good money down on the street,
and where I go, they won't ask to see a receipt.

I moved things around and made a broken-glass trail,
setting up detectives for an epic fail.

I buttoned my coat with the sculpture inside
and took what I thought was a last elevator ride.

But I couldn't resist one more vertical spin.
In the lobby the guy I just nicked got in!

I had to take him up. The point was moot.
I was in the old man's elevator operator suit!

He looked smug and rich, as of yet undeterred.
I said "have a nice night," but I don't think he heard.

My next stop was dark and full of danger.
I could meet my end at the hands of a stranger.

Yet I went by myself, no entourage,
to level 5 of an abandoned parking garage,

Where a black market thrives. Those who dare can score.
It's a criminal village known as Blunderbore.

I know to move slowly. Don't meet anyone's eyes.
I pitched, but couldn't sell my artsy prize.

A gangster whose tongue was forked like a snake,
pulled a knife on me saying my emeralds were fake.

He poked me and sneered: "You come here to play?"
I just shook my head and backed away,

right into a guy who looked out of place.
He was chubby and bald with a middle-aged face.

Here was someone even I could scare.
In a whisper he asked me: *Hey, whatchu-got there?*

He looked like your uncle in a cardigan sweater.
You want money for that, but I've got something better.

With fingers that bent like pudgy machines,
he reached in his pocket. *How about Magic Beans?*

I knew the tall-tales of the "everything drug"
and this guy hardly seemed like a pill-dealing thug.

"Nice try," I told him. "Magic beans don't exist."
And yet – here they are, he beamed, opening his fist.

There were six, brightly colored like the candy kind.
Drugs weren't my thing, and the dude read my mind.

They're not drugs, he told me. *They go in the ground.*
What grows from them turns your whole life around.

An endless supply of unimaginable wealth . . .
"From a plant?" I asked, doubting his mental health.

Only the foolish think the world works one way.
That there are binding laws nature must obey.

If limited experience controls your thoughts,
you won't see what really divides 'haves' and 'have nots'.

His lullaby voice made my head and ears ache.
To trade or walk – which was the bigger mistake?

My mother's confused questions rang in my ear.
Decide, he said gruffly. *Your Mommy's not here.*

Then he softened and gave me his business card.
The logo was blocky, kind of avant-garde.

The words kept shifting, and (sensing my suspicions)
He told me his business was "acquisitions."

I doubted if I'd ever see this guy again.
Not if, he said calmly. *The question is **when**.*

Freaked out by his psychic, parlor trick,
I made the trade, took the beans, and got out quick.

I kept telling myself I had made a good deal.
Money growing on trees was no less real

than apples or oranges, or grapes on the vine.
(A rationalization of my own design.)

I was due home to Mother. In fact, I was late.
Someone in her condition should not have to wait.

She's become sadly and increasingly less aware,
often talking to people who weren't really there.

With Dad gone, her care had fallen solely on me.
Day to day I never knew exactly what I would see.

That night was no different; she was pacing the hall,
going on about a man who had just "come to call."

She said: "Don't wait up. We'll be out late."
Then she asked if the bow in her hair was straight.

She liked fancy talk, so I said "beg your pardon,"
then I slipped out back and put the beans in her garden.

When I came back in she was all aglow,
waiting for a date who wouldn't show.

Regardless, I asked about her evening plan
and what did she like about the mystery man.

Playing along does help keep her calm,
but I was not prepared for this little bomb:

"His sculpture got stolen a few hours ago.
He said you did it, but I told him no!"

I couldn't believe what I'd just heard.
I asked her to tell me, word for word.

Her mood suddenly changed, as it often does.
Now she feared him. She didn't know who that man was.

"What else?" I asked, but her mind was a blur.
Then a knock at the door sparked a memory in her.

She cried in a panic: "He said he'd be back!"
I opened it. The Doc smiled and said:

"Hello, Jack."

PART III

A path of action can present itself
as the only worthwhile endeavor.

Such was the case as I set out to find
this "FoFum" (or "FeeFye". Whatever.)

Once through that door, I knew right away
I'd left the world I'd known.

I was in a forest, but the "trees" were
made of metal, glass and stone.

They looked burnt and broken like targets
in a sci fi movie battle.

As I examined one I heard again
the sound of the spray can rattle.

It came again from deep in the forest.
There was virtually no one around.

No paint-release hiss told me this was a signal.
I was meant to follow the sound.

I didn't like the idea, or the darkness ahead,
but I'd get no welcome mat.

So I started down a path with fear and caution,
clearly the mouse to his cat.

After several minutes I heard the rattle above me.
I looked up and found his shape.

In one of the tree things, his legs dangled
from a perch that looked like a fire escape.

I was about to ask him where to find Jack,
but his own question came down instead:

"Is it true what they say? That you have
the power to bring people back from the dead?"

It took me a second to even process
the gravelly voice that had spoken.

"The brain is science. I learned how it works.
I can fix it when it's broken."

"Can you teach me?" he asked. "I don't like science,
but I'd like to do what you do."

I told him no, but if he had twelve years,
I could point out a college or two.

"I'm looking for Jack," I said, impatient.
"You said you could help in your art."

"I said I could *help*? Or I told *you* to do it?
There's a discrepancy with that part."

I knew I'd have to earn his trust,
or he'd leave, and I'd be done.

When I asked why he went by two different names,
he asked why I used only one.

He told me how impressed he was
that I was able to follow his sign.

I rolled my eyes. Could I just get that kid
to return the thing that was mine?

I wasn't in the mood for compliments
from a split personality elf.

"The good news?" he said. "You're on the right path.
The bad news you'll discover yourself."

The laughter that followed had a spookiness
that caught me a little off guard.

With a flick of his wrist, he tossed
at me what looked like an index card.

It fluttered down, but I couldn't catch it.
It landed at my feet.

When I picked it up, I found myself
back on the late-night city street.

The elf was gone, but I heard his voice
echo, coaching me to "be good."

On the card was a handwritten address
in a sketchy neighborhood.

The stolen sculpture had taken a back seat
to the principle involved.

I would visit this place, and one way or another
my case would be resolved.

No cab would stop, so I went underground
and took a filthy subway east.

I was accosted on the train by an elderly man
who was dressed like a voodoo priest.

He smelled like a dumpster, and his hollow eyes
were set deep behind matted hair.

In a panic he yelled about the "End of Days"
and how I should prepare.

At my stop, it was all I could do
to duck out through the sliding door.

Still trying to hold my attention,
the lunatic thumped on the window and swore.

This cast of unusual characters
had me frightened, I must confess.

And none was stranger than the woman
who opened the door at Jack's address.

She had the distracted look of someone
certifiably loony.

Odder still, her eyes went wide and
she acted as if she knew me.

She gasped and touched her face with
fingers that couldn't have been much thinner.

She said I was early. She wasn't yet ready
to be taken out to dinner.

I said I was there to speak with Jack,
and added: "You must be his mother."

According to her they'd spent years
in this place taking care of one another.

As I suspected, she wasn't too happy
to hear Jack had committed a crime.

She insisted that was nonsense and rushed
to get ready, looking pressed for time.

One minute she flirted and talked of our date.
Perhaps we could see a show.

The next she got frightened, called me
an intruder and demanded that I go.

Knowing her condition, I calmly suggested
we relax and take a seat.

That's when I heard the spray can rattle,
calling me back to the street.

I said I'd return to speak with her son,
but she'd turned off her fragile mind.

I ran out the door and followed the sound,
not knowing what message I'd find.

FeeFye had sprayed in his silver white:

above my head.

Then it slowly changed to

in FoFum's black and red.

PART IV

It made no sense that he was standing there.
I tried to look like I didn't care.

"You stole from me. Now give it back."
But I didn't have his stupid knick knack.

That wasn't at all what he wanted to hear.
The veins in his temples began to appear.

"Look … I sold it, alright? It's gone."
Then Mom interrupted: "Now you just hang on…

I'm canceling our date. You should just leave!"
She pulled on his pricey jacket sleeve.

I fished out the card that weirdo gave me.
"This is who bought it. Now just let us be."

"Nice try. Get the cash. You're coming along,
or the cops will know everything you've done wrong."

Mom burst out laughing, though it wasn't that funny
when I confessed I wasn't paid in money.

Sick of what he called my "juvenile tricks,"
He said the card was from a Motel 6!

To me the card was gibberish. I didn't need it.
I was surprised when the doctor could easily read it.

"Apparently your buyer is in Room 43.
Get your coat. Like I said, you're coming with me."

There was a dark kind of threat in the doctor's voice.
He found me. I was busted. I had no choice.

He tried to hail a cab unsuccessfully.
So I stuck out my hand, and one stopped for me.

In the backseat I apologized for what I had done.
Then he made the mistake of calling me "son."

He just did it to be nice and help set things right.
I didn't want to go there, but I hated this night.

When I told him, I tried not to look too sad.
The elevator guy from his place was my Dad.

With Mom going crazy, I was scared and alone.
I wasn't telling him this so that he might condone

my actions. That would be asking a lot.
But his look said I hit a compassionate spot.

He said I could get Mom the care she needed,
but not from prison. (A fact I conceded.)

I declared once was enough. I was through with crime.
He said: "Let's take this night one task at a time."

The motel was a dump off an unused road,
failing (I imagined) every building code.

Showing up at the door of a dangerous man
suddenly felt like an epically stupid plan.

I stopped, but he scoffed at my hesitation.
"The business card he gave you was an invitation."

At the door we heard rummaging that was almost violent.
Doc knocked, and the room fell suddenly silent.

The door opened the width of the inside chain.
He looked us over and said just one word: *Explain*.

"Something of mine is in your possession.
If you'd kindly return it, I promise discretion."

He asked if our visit was some kind of joke.
The door slammed shut as the doctor spoke:

"I'll call the police," he said, but to our surprise,
he'd undone the chain, and waved us in with his eyes.

He looked like a salesman on endless commute
in his ill-fitting, pin-striped business suit.

Name's Bernie. So what do I owe this pleasure?
Doc ignored him as he looked around for his treasure.

But the room was clean. Bernie was packed to go.
Doc sat in a chair and said: "I think you know."

It doesn't work like that, was the saleman's reply.
"What doesn't?" asked Doc, making Bernie sigh.

He asked me while rubbing his balding head:
For real? This guy doesn't know he's dead?

"Whoa! What?!" said Doc. "Is that a threat?"
Sorry. My bad. You're not dead yet.

Doc stood up. He was done being polite.
So you've had what you'd call a normal night?

"Perhaps you can tell me what this is about."
(I kept quiet and listened, trying not to freak out.)

*There's a defense mechanism one's mind can craft.
You fell down your building's elevator shaft.*

You were spared the horror. "Wait. That's not true."
That's why no one in the lobby paid attention to you.

Then Bernie asked me to step outside -
which was annoying. What did these guys have to hide?

I stood there, waiting in the freezing cold.
Hoping that sculpture wasn't all that I sold.

A junkie stumbled up to a windowless van,
as I heard the rattle of a graffitist's spray paint can.

PART V

Although the kid had stepped outside,
I refrained from using profanity.

This Bernie character in his business suit
was, to me, a new kind of insanity.

"So you're . . . Death?" I asked him respectfully.
He sure didn't look the part.

He was better suited to show market trends
in a PowerPoint presentation chart.

I'm not "the" Death; I'm "a" Death, he told me plainly.
We have an enormous department.

*I got lucky. I would never have been allowed
to go inside your apartment.*

*I was supposed to "acquire" your surgery patient,
but thanks to your expertise,*

*I could miss my quota. My boss has been on me.
I haven't had a moment's peace.*

I didn't understand – or believe – his nonsense.
  I wasn't sure what he planned to divulge.

I asked him: "I know that you're pressed for time,
  but perhaps you could . . . indulge?"

He looked at his watch and sat down with a sigh.
  That kid out there gave me your soul.

  Everyone has one, and taking's my job.
  Acquisitions (and damage control).

He told me my night seemed like an ordeal,
  but in real-world, living time,

Not one moment had passed since I'd left
  my home and the scene of the crime.

I'm sorry about this. Seems you got a raw deal,
  But I have to take someone through.

  I don't have the power to take a life,
  but I can't say the same for you.

I don't like deals, but I'll let you decide,
  although time is getting shorter.

Someone is coming to check in with me.
I'm not missing my bonus this quarter.

I told him I needed a minute alone,
and went into the bathroom to think.

I'd splash some cold water on my face
(provided there was a working sink).

I didn't want him to think I was plotting
an escape, or even trying to stall.

But when I flicked on the light, I froze in shock.
FeeFye had painted the wall.

was written in a smaller version
of his signature letter design.

But the mirror reflected FoFum's message:

The decision was mine.

I did the water on the face thing as best I could,
given the thoughts running through my head.

If I wanted my life back I'd have to put
Jack in my place of being dead.

It was all so simple, a real no-brainer,
when contemplated in the abstract.

But moving from theory to practice was different.
I could never commit such an act.

Now that I knew Jack's situation
I couldn't just judge him a punk.

Knowing my life had already ended,
I wept as my heavy heart sunk.

Back out in the room Bernie buckled
the clasp of his old, worn-down suitcase.

I didn't have to tell him my choice to die.
He could read it on my face.

He gave me a gentle, solemn nod
and kept quiet out of respect.

I followed him out, but passing the threshold
had an unexpected effect.

I was suddenly walking into my building.
My long-time home address.

Someone said "bless you." The crowded lobby
was the same noisy, bustling mess.

Given what I now knew, this no longer
looked like a robbery investigation.

I made my way to the elevator with a
mind-numbing trepidation.

Once there I saw my own broken body
being lifted onto a gurney.

While two paramedics did their best,
I looked around for Bernie.

Instead I saw someone walking toward
me. I knew who it was at first glance.

It was Jack's father, the garden gnome,
in a kind of hypnotic trance.

His sadness was evident, not just on his
cheek, which showed the track of a tear.

He seemed to look right at me as he said:
"My God! What happened here?"

Before I could speak, some man
behind me gave a somber reply.

"The penthouse doctor. Some malfunction.
What a horrible way to die!"

As the gnome removed his hat
and bowed his head in silent prayer,

I realized the old man couldn't see me.
He was *alive*, like the others there.

He was a testament to all that was good
about his dignified working class.

He said: "My first day off in thirteen years,
and this is what comes to pass."

This confirmation felt like a punch to
the face. That little punk thief had lied!

I stormed back out and was back
in the motel lot by Bernie's side.

He stole from you, too. And caused your death.
Not sure why you cut him that slack.

I wasn't in the mood for sarcastic reminders.
"I changed my mind. You can take Jack."

Bernie chuckled and waved his finger,
which was enough to communicate

that my impulsively constructed, alternate
plan was more than a little too late.

For a second time, Bernie made me an offer.
This one more "loophole" than deal.

I wasn't too sure at first when he told me,
though it had a certain appeal.

As far as getting my revenge on Jack,
this seemed one of the better ways.

I could haunt him as a ghoulish ghost
for the rest of his natural days.

So that's what I've been doing ever since
that night. I've driven the poor boy mad.

(And by the way, I learned from these hauntings
that Jack never knew his dad.)

One strange thing: it seems after I died
Jack and his mom became wealthy.

A new house and expert, live-in care
kept his mother happy and healthy.

*   *   *

You've heard the story of a giant
with treasures who lived up in the sky.

And a boy named Jack who stole from him
after "innocently" happening by.

The giant, of course, dies from a nasty fall
while Jack and his mother get rich.

Now that you know what really happened,
it's up to you to decide which

tale you believe and which you'll tell
when you have your next opportunity.

Will you dismiss what is popular and be the
one to enlighten your listening community?

I ask this as if it matters to me, but
I can honestly say I don't care.

Where I am now, we don't get caught up
in what is and isn't fair.

Just keep in mind when you hear
any story on this or another day:

There may be a better than average chance
that it didn't really happen that way.

The End

ACKNOWLEDGEMENTS

———————

I'd like to thank everyone involved in the creation of this book. Special thanks to Dr. Robert Mullin, Dr. Louis Rentz & Lorraine Rentz for their generous contributions toward print production.

On the creative side, special thanks to John Skewes for his time and considerable talents, and also to Christy Futernick for her editorial eye throughout the process.

8: The Untold Story Comic Book

———————————————

Please enjoy on the next several pages a sneak peek at the work-in-progress, comic book version of Creepy the 8th Dwarf's previously untold story.

THE STORIES WE PASS DOWN
                    FROM PARENT TO CHILD

WERE ONCE FILLED WITH DARKNESS,
        BUT SOMEHOW TURNED MILD.
WE TWEAK AND REVISE, AND WHEN ALL ELSE FAILS
WE CHOOSE TO OMIT CERTAIN CRUCIAL DETAILS.
UNTIL THEY'RE FORGOTTEN, AND NOBODY KNOWS
HOW A STORY ORIGINALLY, TRUTHFULLY GOES.

TAKE SNOW WHITE, FOR EXAMPLE. A POPULAR TALE
WITH PLENTY OF UNPLEASANT TRUTHS TO UNVEIL.
FOR INSTANCE, I'D WAGER THAT YOU DIDN'T KNOW
        SEVEN LIVED IN THAT COTTAGE

... WHILE ONE LIVED BELOW.

IT WAS NO USE. WE HAD NOTHING IN COMMON, AND THE PLACE WAS PRETTY SMALL. A GUY CAN ONLY TRY SO HARD WITH SEVEN LOUSY ROOMMATES.

IF WE PUT SOMETHING UNDERNEATH, IT WON'T SOUND SO ... YOU KNOW ... FANCY.

WHAT'S WRONG WITH FANCY?

BEATS ME.

I'D LIKE TO PUT HIM UNDERNEATH.

...MBLE...

HMPH!!

HUH?

GRUMBLE...

SO I STARTED KEEPING TO MYSELF, WHICH PROBABLY MADE THINGS WORSE, I KNOW. BUT I WASN'T THE ONE WITH THE PROBLEM.

Michael Mullin lives in Pasadena, California, although all his sports allegiances remain in his native New England. In addition to *TaleSpins*, he is the co-author of the successful *Larry Gets Lost™* picture book series.

He lives with his wife and their 12-year-old twins, who pretty much run his life, despite his best efforts to appear as if *he* is running *theirs*.